The Eagle and the Seagulls

A Wisdom Story for Children and Adults

James L. Capra

ISBN: 978-1-4834-2791-1 (sc)
ISBN: 978-1-4834-2790-4 (hc)
ISBN: 978-1-4834-2792-8 (e)

Library of Congress Control Number: 2015903896

Because of the dynamic nature of the Internet, any web addresses or links contained in this book may have changed since publication and may no longer be valid. The views expressed in this work are solely those of the author and do not necessarily reflect the views of the publisher, and the publisher hereby disclaims any responsibility for them.

Any people depicted in stock imagery provided by Thinkstock are models, and such images are being used for illustrative purposes only.
Certain stock imagery © Thinkstock.

Lulu Publishing Services rev. date: 03/25/2015

For all those who are going and will go through the storms that life brings.

Foreword

It is a great pleasure to be invited to write a foreword to James L. Capra's latest book. His friend since we were teenagers, I've been witness to over four decades of his unrelenting passion for the most important issues of life: faith, family, integrity, courage, leadership, and success. His accomplishments speak for themselves. He is a rare and extraordinary person, possessing exceptional depth of understanding and fiery conviction. Add to that his natural talent for communicating, plus the drive to make a difference, and you begin to find out why Capra is a leader of leaders who writes with clarity, wit, and wisdom.

An entertaining contemporary parable, *The Seagulls and the Eagle* challenges the reader to prepare for the serious mission of life. Insightful and highly original, the story is a powerful metaphor for the value of *living with foresight and purpose* in a culture obsessed with frivolity. During this time in history when so many tempting elements are in play, all competing for the attention of young people, James L. Capra perfectly describes the attitude necessary to not only weather the storms of life but rise above and experience victory in the midst.

Rev. Robert A. Engelhardt
Pastor, author, speaker

2

Acknowledgments

This book would not have been possible without the love, encouragement, and support of my biggest advocate and fan: my wife, Shelly. For well over three decades, she has constantly sought to bring about the very best in the gifts that have been given to me; she is the very definition of Proverbs 31!

I am extremely thankful to be the father of six outstanding children, who continue to hold me up in their prayers and have loved me and forgiven me for my shortfalls as a father. As young children, they listened intently to this story over and over again as we poured wisdom and prayer into each of their young lives. Throughout the years, my wife and I have watched with great pride as each of them has weathered storms in their lives with courage, strength, and unconditional faith; no father could be prouder.

Finally, I am incredibly thankful to serve my Lord, the God of second chances, who throughout my journey, through some of the fiercest storms I have faced, never abandoned or forsook me. I continue to be astounded by how blessed I have been, and I credit any success that I have to a God who simply loves His children.

Micah was unusually quiet as he sat on the back porch of Grandpa's house. Micah always loved going to his grandpa's house. He enjoyed sitting on the back porch and listening to Grandpa tell stories while they looked at different birds that ate from the bird feeders in the backyard.

"What's wrong?" asked Grandpa.

"Just some school stuff," Micah said quietly.

"School stuff, huh? Sounds sort of serious," said Grandpa.

Micah explained, "It's just that there are these kids, and they are the real popular kids. They think they're better than everyone else!"

"Oh, I see," said Grandpa.

"They always try to get me to hang out with them, but ..." Micah's voice trailed off softly.

"But," said Grandpa, "they are troublemakers—is that it?"

"Yes, sir, and since I won't hang out with them, they make fun of me when I go by them in the hall," Micah said quietly.

"Ah, that can be kind of hurtful," Grandpa said while leaning back in his rocking chair.

"I try to pray about it, Grandpa, but I don't think God's listening to me."

Grandpa leaned forward in his rocking chair and stroked Micah's cheek. "Micah, you remind me of the story about the mighty eagle!" Grandpa exclaimed.

"What is that story about, Grandpa?" Micah asked.

Grandpa began, "Once upon a time, in a land not far from here, on the jagged ridges of a cliff overlooking the great sea, there lived a flock of seagulls. These particular gulls were not very well behaved and would always put off their chores in order to play and have fun. As a matter of fact, the gulls were known to all the other animals that lived on the cliff as the popular group. Several of the other animals liked playing with the gulls because they thought it made them look important and cool.

9

"One bright, sunny afternoon, the cliff gulls got together to play games. They invited only their special friends to play with them. In the midst of all the games, one of the gulls said, 'Hey, we should invite the eagle; he looks pretty cool, and I heard he was really tough too!'

"Now, the eagle lived at the very top of the cliff. His nest was very large, and it looked out over the great sea below. The seagulls were chattering back and forth with each other, and they decided to send one of their own to fly up and invite the eagle to their party.

"One of the gulls flew and flew up the jagged side of the cliff toward the great eagle's nest. As the gull landed next to the edge of the nest, he saw the eagle working very busily on tightening up the edges of the nest. Catching his breath, the seagull waited for the eagle to notice him. Besides, why wouldn't the eagle notice him? He was one of the popular gulls.

"But the eagle ignored the gull and continued to work on his nest.

"Finally, the gull yelled out, 'Hey, eagle! Hey … *eagle!* Me and my friends are getting together to play, and we want you to come down and play with us!'

"The eagle turned briefly to look at the seagull and then turned back to working on the large nest.

13

"The gull looked puzzled and shouted again, 'Hey, hey, eagle, are you deaf? I said you're invited to our party, so come on down!'

"At that, the eagle moved slowly toward the seagull, pointed to the horizon out over the great sea, and said calmly, 'There is a storm coming.'

"The gull was puzzled as he looked up into the clear, blue sky and out toward the sunny horizon. The gull cried out, 'Are you crazy? What storm? There's not a cloud in the sky!' The gull went on to say, 'Listen, eagle, we only invite our special friends to play with us, so if you don't come down, all the others will think you're weird!'

"The eagle looked over at the gull and once again pointed to the horizon, saying, 'There is a storm coming.'

17

"The seagull began to get angry with the eagle, because he thought the eagle was making excuses not to come down and play with the other gulls. While the eagle went back to tending to his nest, the gull began to make fun of him. He said, 'I guess you're not as cool or tough as everyone says!' The gull began to laugh and squawk. 'Hey, eagle, as a matter of fact, you're pretty weird for a big, tough bald eagle! I bet your parents are weird too, and—'

"But before the seagull could utter another word, the eagle stretched out his mighty wing, pointed to the horizon, glared at the gull, and said sternly, 'There is a storm coming!'

"At that, the gull swallowed hard and flew back down the cliff to tell all the others what the eagle had said. At once, all of the seagulls and some of the other cliff creatures laughed and laughed. They pointed to the eagle and mocked him and his work on the nest. They called him names, hurled insults at him, and even made fun of his family. But all the while, the seagulls and their playmates hadn't noticed that the wind had shifted. Just then, dark clouds began to move in as the great sea churned its waves against the rocks below.

21

"As the storm grew, the creatures began to get scared. They cried out, 'What do we do? Where can we hide?' But it was too late. The mighty storm had arrived, and the wind pounded the cliff. The seagulls tried to fly away, but the wind was too strong. They began to panic as they ran toward the edge of the cliff in the blinding rain.

"Far up on the cliff, the mighty eagle stepped up onto the edge of the great nest while the storm raged on. As the wind grew stronger and fiercer, the eagle dug his golden talons into the edge of the nest. When the storm was at its mightiest, when the wind roared so hard that it shook the very cliff itself, the eagle raised both of his wings while peering into the heart of the storm and all at once released his grip.

"As the wind blew harder, the eagle soared faster and faster, going higher and higher without ever having to flap his wings. All at once, he found himself flying high above the storm in the warmth of the sun above. As the eagle soared majestically, he could see in the distance—to his right and left—other eagles gliding above the storm, all bathed in the warm sunlight.

"When the storm subsided, the eagle flew back toward his nest. As he approached the great nest, he saw below only feathers and fur where the seagulls and other animals had once played."

Grandpa put his hand on Micah's shoulder and looked directly into his eyes. "You are the eagle, Micah," he said as he squeezed Micah's shoulder firmly. "I believe God is teaching you how to go through the different storms in your life. You see, Micah, we all want God to solve our problems as soon as they arise. We get frustrated and sometimes angry when He doesn't show up right away." He continued softly, "God wants to take us through the storms so that we may learn how to be patient, and most of all, trust Him."

Micah nodded. "I think I understand, Grandpa."

Grandpa jumped out of his rocking chair and said, "That reminds me, I have something for you!" He opened his big photo album, pulled out a picture, and gave it to Micah. "Use this to remind you of the lesson of the eagle."

"Thanks, Grandpa. This is so great!"

At school the next day, Micah began his first class by opening up his binder. On the inside cover was the picture Grandpa had given him. Micah smiled as he gazed at the picture and began his class.

"Those who wait on the Lord will renew their strength, they will run and not be weary, they will mount up on wings of eagles" (Isaiah 40:31).

Things for the Reader to Consider:

1. We all face storms in our lives. Storms take on different shapes in different circumstances. Maybe you are facing a difficult time with a friend or friends, or a family member is causing some difficulty.

2. Storms can also be personal struggles we face. Some struggles include problems with studies, or problems with drugs, alcohol, tobacco, or relationships.

3. Sometimes you may think that only you are going through this struggle, and you might feel very alone. You question where God is and wonder if He hears your prayer, your cries for help.

4. We want God to take us out of the storm because of our fear of the turmoil in the storm or because of embarrassment that the particular storm brings.

Consider that God promises He will never forsake us or leave us; even in the midst of the fiercest storm, God is with His children. Sometimes it is necessary to go through a great storm so that we will become stronger and more mature in our walk. Consider the eagle in this story. He knew a storm was coming, and he was preparing for it. An eagle's nest can weigh several hundred pounds and is so well crafted that it can withstand up to hurricane-force winds. Eagles are trained early on how to build their nests so that they will withstand storms and provide protection for their young.

When a storm comes, eagles don't sit in their nests; in fact, they are known to step out on the edge of the nest and use the storm's winds to fly to heights far above the storm clouds. So they actually use the strength of the storm to help them rise above it. The eagle knows he will be bounced around in the storm, but he is confident that he was made to face the storm and built to withstand anything the storm brings. He knows instinctively that he will only go through the rough part for just a little while and then soon be soaring above the storm, bathed in the warmth of the sun. And it is the same with us; when a storm comes, we may have to go through the fiercest part for a little while, but soon we will be bathed in the warmth of the true Son!

About the Author

James L. Capra is the CEO and founder of The Front Line Leadership Group, a leadership training and development firm located in Argyle, Texas. Mr. Capra is also the author of *Leadership at the Front Line: Lessons Learned About Loving, Leading, and Legacy from a Warrior and Public Servant,* published by Lulu. Jimmy, as he is known by his friends and colleagues, retired in August 2014 after more than twenty-seven years with the Drug Enforcement Administration. Prior to his retirement, Jimmy served as the chief of global operations, responsible for 227 domestic offices and eighty-six foreign offices in sixty-seven countries. Prior to his DEA career, Jimmy served in the US Navy, US Navy Reserves, Air National Guard, and as a military intelligence officer. He holds a bachelor of science from Marist College and a master of education from Seton Hall University.

To contact him for speaking engagements, e-mail him at jlcapra@yahoo.com or via his website, *www.FrontLineLeadershipGroup.com.*

Made in the USA
Lexington, KY
30 September 2015